Flip through the pages to see a hungry wolf!

This Book Belongs To

. . . .

Text copyright © 1998 Vivian French
Illustrations copyright © 1998 David Melling

This edition first published 1998
by Hodder Children's Books

The right of Vivian French and David Melling to be
identified as the Author and Illustrator of the Work has
been asserted by them in accordance with the Copyright,
Designs and Patents Act 1988.

10   9   8   7   6   5   4   3

A Catalogue record for this book is available from the
British Library

ISBN 0340 71359 3

Printed and bound in Great Britain by
The Devonshire Press, Torquay, Devon TQ2 7NX

Hodder Children's Books
A Division of Hodder Headline plc
338 Euston Road
London NW1 3BH

Iggy Pig's Party

Vivian French

Illustrated by David Melling

Hodder
Children's
Books

a division of Hodder Headline plc

For Joe
With much love
Vivie

For Liberty Bennett
D.M.

It was Iggy Pig's birthday.

"Mother Pig, Mother Pig!" said
Iggy Pig. "Can I have a party
at four o'clock today?"

1

"Oink," said Mother Pig.
"You are my own dear Iggy Pig.
Of course you may have a party."

"HURRAH!" said Iggy Pig.
"HURRAH!"

He went dancing around
the farmyard.
"I'm going to have a party!
I'm going to have a party!
I'm going to have a party
at four o'clock today!"

Behind the hedge was
a big grey animal.
A big grey animal with
a long bushy tail.

"AHA!" said the big grey
animal.
"AHA!" and he smiled a
hungry smile.

Tabby Cat heard Iggy Pig
singing.
"Meeow! Meeow!" said
Tabby Cat.
"Are you going to invite me
to your party, Iggy Pig?"

"Oh YES, Tabby Cat,"
said Iggy Pig. "Of course
you can come to my party!"

"Meeow! Meeow!" said
Tabby Cat.
"I hope you will have a
slippery fish for me to eat!"

"Oh YES, Tabby Cat,"
said Iggy Pig.
"There will be a BIG
slippery fish."

"Good," said Tabby Cat.
"Then I'll come."

Iggy Pig went dancing
around the farmyard.
"I'm going to have a party!
I'm going to have a party!
I'm going to have a party
at four o'clock today!"

Behind the wall was the big
grey animal.
The big grey animal with
the long bushy tail.
The big grey animal with
the hungry smile.

"AHA!" said the big grey
animal, and his tummy rumbled.

Dusty Dog heard Iggy Pig
singing.
"Woof! Woof!" said Dusty Dog.
"Are you going to invite me
to your party, Iggy Pig?"

"Oh YES, Dusty Dog,"
said Iggy Pig. "Of course
you can come to my party!"

"Woof! Woof!" said Dusty Dog.
"I hope there will be a big juicy
bone for me to eat!"

"Oh YES, Dusty Dog,"
said Iggy Pig.
"There will be a HUGE
juicy bone."

"Good," said Dusty Dog.
"Then I'll come!"

Iggy Pig went dancing
around the farmyard.
"I'm going to have a party!
I'm going to have a party!
I'm going to have a party
at four o'clock today!"

Behind the fence was the big
grey animal.

The big grey animal with
the long bushy tail.

The big grey animal with
the hungry smile.

The big grey animal with
the rumbling tummy.

"AHA!" said the big grey
animal, and he licked his lips.

Iggy pig danced
all the way home.
"I'm going to have a party!
I'm going to have a party!
I'm going to have a party
at four o'clock today!"

"That's right, my own dear
Iggy Pig," said Mother Pig.
"We will have cabbage leaves
to crunch.
We will have potato peelings
to munch.
We will sing Happy Birthday
to you!"

"Mother Pig, Mother Pig!"
said Iggy Pig.
"We must have a BIG
slippery fish for Tabby Cat!"

Mother Pig shook her head.
"Dear me, Iggy Pig. Where
would we find a slippery fish?
Cabbage leaves are MUCH
nicer!"

19

"We must have a HUGE
juicy bone for Dusty Dog!"

Mother Pig shook her head.
"Dear me, Iggy Pig. Where
would we find a juicy bone?
Potato peelings are MUCH
better!"

Iggy Pig went sadly outside.

"I need a BIG slippery fish.
I need a HUGE juicy bone.
I don't want to eat cabbage
leaves all by myself.
I don't want to eat potato
peelings all by myself."

The big grey animal stepped
out from behind a tree.
"AHEM!" he said.

"WHO ARE YOU?"
asked Iggy Pig.

"Just a friend," said
the big grey animal.
"Dear little pig - did you say
you wanted a slippery fish?"
"That's right," said Iggy Pig.

"And, dear little pig - you wanted a big juicy bone?" "Yes please!" said Iggy Pig.

"EASY!" said the
big grey animal.
"I'll fetch them straight away.
Oh - little pig! You will invite
me to your party, won't you?"

"OF COURSE I will!"
said Iggy Pig.

Iggy Pig went dancing
around the farmyard.
"I'm going to have a party!
I'm going to have a party!
I'm going to have a party
at four o'clock today!"

It was five minutes
before four o'clock.

The big grey animal
came up to Iggy Pig.
"Here you are little pig!
Here is the slippery fish!
Here is the juicy bone!
Eat them up quickly!
Eat them up quickly
and get FAT!"

"Oh NO!" said Iggy Pig.
"*I* don't like slippery fish.
I don't like juicy bones.
I like cabbage leaves
and potato peelings.
What do *you* like
big grey animal?"

The big grey animal
licked his lips.

The big grey animal's
tummy rumbled.

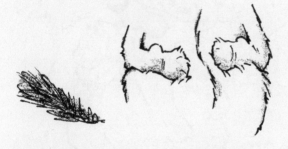

The big grey animal
smiled his hungry smile.
"I like - LITTLE PIGS!"
he said, and he JUMPED . . .

JUST as Dusty Dog
and Tabby Cat
came around the corner.

"WOOF! WOOF! WOOF!"
barked Dusty Dog.
He showed his sharp white teeth.

"MEEEOW! MEEEOW!"
meowed Tabby Cat.
She showed her sharp
shiny claws.

"WOWLY! WOWLY!"
howled the big grey animal.

He turned right round
and he ran . . .

He ran and he ran and
he ran . . .

"Four o'clock!"
said Iggy Pig.
"Time for my party!"

Tabby Cat ate her
BIG slippery fish.
Dusty Dog crunched
his HUGE juicy bone.

Iggy Pig crunched cabbage
leaves, and munched potato
peelings until he was all
filled up . . .

And they all sang Happy
Birthday to you!

Iggy Pig went to bed that night
feeling very full and happy.
"That was the best party ever!"
he said.

"Indeed it was, my own dear
Iggy Pig," said Mother Pig.
"It was so clever of you
to find a slippery fish *and*
a juicy bone."

"Oh," said Iggy Pig.
"I didn't find them.
The big grey animal did."
And he yawned a great big
yawn.

"OINK!" said Mother Pig.
"OINK! OINK! OINK!
Iggy Pig! Iggy Pig! Have you
been talking to a WOLF?"

Iggy Pig didn't answer.
Iggy Pig was fast asleep.

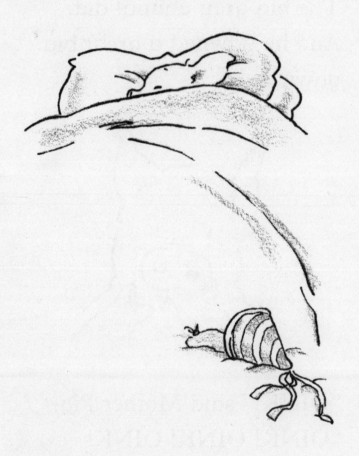